POD FIFTEEN

PHILIP HARRIS

Pod Fifteen

by Philip Harris

Copyright © 2018 by Philip Harris
All rights reserved.

Pod Fifteen originally appeared in Canyons of the Damned Issue 14 published by Holt Smith Limited

ISBN 978-0-9938998-8-1 (Print)

ISBN 978-0-9938998-9-8 (Ebook)

10 9 8 7 6 5 4 3 2 1

First Edition

Cover design by Damonza

Published by Philip Harris

http://www.SolitaryMindset.com

For the dead

1
———

ELLIS STARED AT THE FACE OF THE DEAD MAN AND TRIED TO guess his name. "How about Danny?"

Incorrect.

"Really? He looks like a Danny to me. Or a Pete. Either Pete or Sid."

Both Pete and Sid are incorrect.

"All right, I give in."

The subject's name was Marcus Wilson.

"Okay, a Marcus. That sounds like a salesman's name. Probably sold real estate or something."

Marcus Wilson was a motivational speaker for the Trigenics Corporation.

"See? He was selling people a better life. One point to me. How many does that make now?"

You have earned three points since leaving Denia.

"That's a record."

Correct.

"Right, now for the important bit." Ellis ran his fingers through his greasy hair. He couldn't remember when he'd last showered. "He looks pretty pale, even for a dead guy. Probably died due to loss of blood somehow. He get stabbed by an irate customer?"

Incorrect.

"Hit by a car?"

Incorrect.

"Suicide."

Incorrect.

Ellis sighed. "Okay, how did this one bite the dust?"

Marcus Wilson was killed in a skiing accident. Primary cause of death was epidural hematoma.

Ellis winced. "Ouch."

He considered kicking off another round of the game, but he was tired, and his hands were shaking slightly. He switched off the display.

"Lisa, confirm travel time."

It has been three weeks, six hours, fifty-two minutes, and seventeen seconds since we left the station.

"Three weeks, huh? In that case, I think it must be time to switch up your vocal settings. Let's try female this time. Just pick something at random and give me a test phrase."

Understood.

Welcome aboard the Deep Space Transport Vessel Redhawk, Pilot Osako.

Ellis winced. "No, I don't think so. That sounds too much like my ex-wife. Try something a bit more girl next door."

I do not understand, girl next door.

"You know: nice, polite, intelligent. The sort of girl my mom would have wanted me to marry."

A pause.

Welcome aboard the Deep Space Transport Vessel Redhawk, Pilot Osako.

Ellis smiled. "That's more like it. Accept."

Vocal Option Three Eighty-four selected.

The console in front of Ellis let out a low buzz. A red light flickered on for a few seconds, then went dark again.

"Lisa, run a diagnostics sweep. Let's make sure this pile of junk is going to get us where we're going."

Beginning internal diagnostics.

"Thank you. I'll be in my executive suite. Don't wake me unless the ship catches fire."

Understood.

Ellis climbed out of the pilot's chair, opened the door to his quarters, and walked inside. The door juddered almost closed behind him. He kicked the lower corner and it lurched the final couple of inches. The room was just over twenty feet long and half as wide, just enough room for a bunk and a small metal locker that served as his closet, pantry, and bookshelf. A second door, this one barely wide enough to qualify as one, led into the bathroom with its shower and fold-out sink. It was one of the few things on the Redhawk that could actually be considered a luxury.

An almost-empty bottle of bourbon stood on the floor beside the narrow strip of foam that served as his mattress. The foam sat on top of a sheet of metal welded to the outer hull. When he tried to sleep, he could feel the vibration of the ship's engines. He grabbed the bottle and shook it, then sighed and sat down. Three weeks in and he was down to the last quarter of the bourbon. At least he had other, more inventive ways to numb the tedium.

He lay back on the bed, the bourbon clutched to his chest like a teddy bear. The last pilot had taped a poster of some model Ellis didn't recognize to the ceiling. Its ink had faded until the man's pale-blue eyes were almost completely white, and a corner curled up where one of the tacks had come free. Ellis had found the tack in his bed halfway through his first night, but not bothered to push it back in.

The hull beside his head groaned. He still wasn't used to the sound. No, scratch that. He was used to it; he was just convinced it was a sign that the Redhawk was going to disintegrate before they reached Kiran. If that happened, he wondered whether the Denians would dispatch some sort of cleanup crew to pick up the ship's cargo and take it on to their beloved burial planet. And if they did, would they take his body along as well? Just for good measure?

He pinched the bridge of his nose. A familiar high-pitched whine was just creeping into his consciousness. In half an hour, it would settle in at the edge of his hearing— just too loud for him to ignore. There it would sit, gradually driving him insane until he grabbed the nearest sharp implement and jammed it into his brains to scratch that infuriating, tinnitus-derived itch.

Unless he took his medicine.

He held up the bottle of bourbon. Alcohol had long since stopped having any real effect on him. There just wasn't enough weight allowance on a long-haul job to bring enough to manage anything beyond a mild buzz. He'd brought the bourbon out of a misplaced sense of nostalgia rather than anything else.

The tinnitus grew stronger, drowning out the distant rumble of the Redhawk's engines for a few seconds before fading away again. It would be back.

Ellis sat up on the edge of the bunk and opened the locker door. If he needed to, he could reach the back of it from where he was sitting, but he kept his medicine close at hand. He stood the bourbon on the floor, just inside the locker, and pulled a wooden box from a shelf.

The box's surface was scratched and worn, and the smell

of the cigars it had once held was almost gone, but he only really cared about what was inside it. He flipped the lid and smiled when he saw the familiar envelopes—tiny squares barely bigger than his thumbnail. They were made of paper so thin you could see the shadows of their contents if you held them up to the light. The front of each one was painted with an intricate, abstract pattern that told connoisseurs like Ellis the exact pedigree of the medicine they were handling. They were works of art, really.

He flicked through the envelopes, looking for the blue stamp of his favorite brand. If he'd had the money, he'd have stocked up on more, but he'd get through a lot of medicine in three and a half months. The Trigenics Corporation weren't paying him that well.

The little stack of what he liked to call *Epic Blue* was at the back of the box—five envelopes. That meant half of it was gone already. He opened his mouth and twisted his jaw from side to side in an effort to dislodge the growing tinnitus. As always, it didn't help.

He removed one of the *Epic Blue* envelopes and placed the box back on the shelf. Sitting back on the bunk, he wiped the palm of his left hand on the rough blanket. Satisfied there was no moisture on it, he carefully squeezed the sides of the envelope until it popped open. Then he tipped the circle of medicine out onto his palm. He knew better than to savor this part of the ritual—he'd ruined more than one dose by letting it stick to his hand. He lifted the paperthin disk to his mouth and lapped it up like a dog.

Closing his eyes, he lay back on the bunk. Heat spread across his tongue. Its progress slowed, and, for a moment, he was afraid he'd been ripped off and it was a bad batch. Then the warmth crept up the inside of his cheeks and across the roof of his mouth. Tendrils of pleasure wormed their way through his body, chasing away the darkness with their light. His heart stuttered and there was the usual instant of panic where his body instinctively feared for its survival. Then his heart resumed its steady beat and his thoughts lit up like fireworks.

2

"Good morning, Lisa."

Good morning, Pilot.

"Diagnostics show up anything interesting?"

The ship is operating at 93.2 percent efficiency. All systems are within acceptable limits. Engine capacity is at seventy-eight percent.

"Good, good."

Ellis brushed his hand across the thick stubble on his chin. The tinnitus had gone for now, and he actually found himself smiling. He jumped into the pilot's seat and pushed off with his feet. The articulated arm that connected the seat to the ceiling carried him across the bridge to the main console and its display screen.

"Bring up the crypt."

The screen flickered to life and revealed the ship's cargo hold.

"Lights."

Two dozen LED lights burst to life, revealing a series of rectangular metal pods laid out in neat rows. Each pod had three large white digits painted on it. There were one hundred and eighty of them in total—the precious, lifeless cargo Ellis was responsible for getting to Kiran in one piece.

Ellis swept his finger over the screen. "Eeny, meeny, miny mo!" He jabbed his finger down. "I'll take corpse number fifty-seven for three points."

The display changed to a close-up of a man's face, dark skinned and deeply lined. He was bald, and the puckered edge of a scar curved around the front of his skull.

"Hm, he looks like a Richard."

Incorrect.

"Are you sure?"

Yes.

"Leroy?"

Incorrect.

"Derek?"

Incorrect. The subject's name is Nathan Meadows.

"He died of a brain tumor or something though, right?"

Correct. A glioblastoma multiforme.

"How old was he? Sixty-three?"

At time of death, he was approximately seventy-one years old.

"Wow, he looks pretty good for his age. Apart from the whole operating-scar thing."

Lisa didn't reply.

"Okay, show me the crypt again."

The display changed back to the rows of metal boxes. The white numbers glowed under the harsh lights.

Ellis studied the screen. "Let's go with number fifteen."

A young Asian woman's face appeared on the screen.

Ellis stared at the image for several long seconds before he spoke. "Her name was Lucy. She was nineteen when she died, a student. She'd just started at college and had gone to a drugstore to stock up on some basics—milk, bread." Ellis took a deep breath. "Some punk-ass kid came in waving a gun around. The owner pulled a shotgun out and tried to shoot the kid. He missed and hit Lucy. She died in the hospital later that night. Alone."

There was a pause.

Incorrect.

Ellis pushed the pilot's chair back to the main control panel. "Turn it off."

As the display died, Ellis stood. Without speaking, he walked slowly into his quarters.

3

Ellis sat in the cargo hold, opposite pod fifteen. He'd never seen inside any of the pods, but from the outside, they looked more like ordinary containers that might carry a shipment of food or electronics. They were just long, rectangular boxes. Each one had a small panel on the outside with a keypad and a single LED that shone green to show the pod's seal was intact.

He stared at the rectangular identification plate riveted to the side of the pod. There was a picture of the woman on it—the kind of bland image that government organizations demanded be captured for passports and driving licenses. Despite the banality of the photograph, there was a noticeable brightness in her eyes—some spark within her hiding just beneath the surface, ready to break out and show itself when the serious photographic business was done.

The panel gave her name, too: Tenshi Kuro. She'd been twenty-four when she died. There was other information— her weight, height, place of birth—but Ellis was drawn to the photograph. He stared at it, afraid to blink, until his eyes began to water.

The bottle of bourbon was sitting on the floor between his legs. He picked it up and took a mouthful, his eyes not leaving the image of the woman in the coffin even as the liquor burned his throat. The bourbon sloshed loudly as he placed it back on the floor. The bottle was almost empty.

Out of the corner of his eye, he saw the LED on the container flicker. His eyes darted to it. He was convinced it had changed color, but it still shone green. The pod was sealed. He felt a pang of disappointment, and, for a few seconds, considered opening it himself. There was a protocol for gaining access to a pod, although he had no idea on what grounds it might be justified. Certainly, he had no reason to disturb the woman's body.

He took another drink, savoring the alcohol's heat and letting it burn away the urge to open the pod. No good could come of that. Tears formed at the corners of his eyes and he tried to convince himself it was just the drink.

"Lisa, run a diagnostics check on pod fifteen, please."

There was a brief pause.

All systems operating within expected ranges. Hermetic seal intact.

Another pause.

As was the case when you made your third enquiry, seventeen minutes ago.

Ellis wiped the back of his hand across his mouth and sniffed. His fingers were trembling. He held his hand up to his face and stared at his fingers, willing them to still. His index finger twitched as if in rebellion. He let his hand drop again.

His fingers sought out the label on the bottle resting between his legs and started peeling it away. His wife had told him once that peeling labels from bottles was a sign of sexual frustration. He smiled sadly at the memory of the passionate rebuttal that had followed. That had been before fate had torn them apart. He squeezed his eyes shut for a few seconds, trying to dislodge the memory. Then he ripped off another scrap of label, rolled it into a ball, and flicked it away. It rebounded off the side of the pod and fell through a gap in the floor.

"I'm sorry." The words came out fragmented. Tears welled in his eyes again. "I'm sorry, Lucy."

Ellis drained the last of the bourbon. A sudden burst of anger hit him, and he sent the bottle flying across the room. It hit the wall and shattered. Shards of glass rained down onto the floor like ice crystals. He let his head drop forward and pressed his hands against his face. They smelled of bourbon and sweat. He sobbed.

He ran his hands down his face and licked his lips. His mouth was gummy, thick with dense saliva. He clenched his hands until his knuckles turned white, then opened them and watched his fingers twitch and shake. Some unseen piece of the ship's mechanisms clunked somewhere beneath the floor. He slid over to the pod and knelt beside it. The LED glowed green. He ran his fingertips lightly over the keypad.

"Lisa, give me the access code for pod fifteen."

Trigenics procedures state that access to cargo pods by contracted employees is prohibited.

"Unless there's an emergency."

I do not detect an emergency situation.

"No, I suppose you don't." Ellis sighed. "Just give me the code."

Trigenics procedures state that access to cargo containers by contracted employees is prohibited. The consequences for unauthorized access include termination of employment and substantial fines.

"I'm overriding the procedure. I'll deal with the consequences."

Understood. Access code 90410756.

Ellis tapped the first seven digits into the keypad. His index finger rested on the final key. He held it there, willing the withdrawal to take the decision away from him, but his finger held steady. He tapped the CANCEL button, and the control panel gave a disgruntled beep.

He ran his fingers over the identification plate, tracing the woman's image. Then he turned and leaned his back against the pod. He tipped his head up and stared into the harsh light above until his eyes began to water and he was forced to look away. Patches of light danced across his vision when he blinked.

"I'm sorry."

He reached into his pocket and pulled out a tiny envelope of *Epic Blue*. His hands shook as he squeezed the edges of the packet and tipped the disk of medicine out onto his palm.

There was no tinnitus yet, but he could feel it circling, biding its time. It would be back before long. He raised his hand and dabbed his tongue against the disk.

The familiar warming sensation spread across his tongue and along the roof of his mouth. He held his breath, waiting for the drug to reach his heart. Even then, when the lurching, hesitant beats came, he felt the same grasping fear he always did. His heart seemed to take an age to settle and enough time passed that he began to wonder if he'd finally pushed his aging body too far. When it finally calmed down, he closed his eyes and let his head fall back against the pod as the drug worked its magic.

4

THREE HOURS LATER, ELLIS CAREFULLY MADE HIS WAY TO THE bridge. The medicine lingered at the back of his mind, and, for the moment, the sharp edges of his memories had been worn smooth. Smooth enough for him to function, anyway. If he concentrated hard enough, he could conjure up the last vestiges of its effects—a gentle tickling of his pleasure sensors and the warm glow of a life well lived.

It took three attempts to get the door to the bridge to open. When it finally did, it let out a grinding, metallic complaint and only opened eighty percent of the way.

"This ship is falling apart."

Sensors indicate all systems are operating within expected parameters.

"Yeah? Well, Trigenics need to adjust their parameters. I'm going to write them a stern letter when we get to Kiran."

I would suggest an electronic form of communication. Routing of physical items is often unreliable.

"Okay, I'll send them an email. Whatever, this rust bucket is past its retirement age." Ellis held up a hand. "Don't bother replying to that. It's just a figure of speech."

Understood.

Ellis climbed into the pilot's chair and kicked off so that it swung around the cabin before returning to the main console. "Start a short-range scan." He paused. "No, wait. We'll do that later." He tapped his fingers against the edge of the console. "Bring up the record for Tenshi Kuro."

The main display changed to the image of the woman in pod fifteen.

"Give me split screen. Put her photograph on segment one."

The display flickered. Her image appeared on the left-hand side. Ellis considered it for a moment before he spoke again. "Access my personal files. Play file *Xmas39* on segment two."

The right side of the display turned black for a few seconds, then a video appeared. It showed an Asian girl of four or five riding a red bicycle along a pathway in a garden. A glittering silver bow was stuck to the handlebars. The bike wavered unsteadily as the girl struggled to keep it upright, but her face was filled with joy. A woman followed along behind, her hands ready to catch the girl if she fell.

The girl squeezed the brakes, and the bike rolled to a halt. It tipped sideways and almost fell, but the girl managed to catch it. Once the bike was under control, she looked up at the camera and waved. The woman behind the girl clapped her hands and grinned, almost as excited as the girl herself.

There was a cut, and the video changed to show the girl riding away from the camera. The woman was standing beside the path, still smiling. The camera tilted down and then the video restarted.

"Play file *Sept54*."

The video of the girl on the bike was replaced by a shot

of a car laden down with boxes. A young woman was pushing a sleeping bag into the car's trunk, crushing it between two bulging suitcases.

"Bring up the sound."

A man's laughter came from somewhere near the camera. "Are you sure you're taking enough stuff, Lucy?"

The woman from the first video, older now, came into view. "Leave her alone."

"Yeah, Dad," said Lucy, "leave me alone. It's my comfort blanket."

"I know, and those are your two dozen comfort dresses, your comfort makeup kit, and your comfort pots and pans."

Lucy tilted her head and stuck her tongue out at the camera.

The video cut to another angle, showing Lucy standing beside the car.

The older woman walked into view. "Are you sure you don't want to take some food? We've got plenty."

"We have comfort milk," said the male voice.

Lucy rolled her eyes. "No, I'll pick some up when I get there."

"Well, if you're su—"

"I'm sure. I need to get going."

The older woman sighed and held her arms wide. Lucy stepped into them and they hugged.

"We could come with you," said the woman.

"No, I'll be fine."

"All right, well, you take care, honey."

"I will, Mom. I promise."

The woman sighed and blinked away tears, then released her grip.

Lucy stepped back and swung open the driver's door.

A cough came from behind the camera. "Aren't you forgetting something?"

Lucy frowned and looked up into the sky, her finger pressed against her chin as though she was deep in thought. "No, I don't think so..."

"Lucy..."

Lucy grinned. "Oh yeah, the old man wants a hug, too." She turned and held her arms out.

The video cut again. Lucy was sitting in the driver's seat and the engine was running.

"I'm going to miss her," said the older woman.

"Me too," said the man, "but we'll see her again next weekend."

Lucy turned and waved at the camera.

"Pause and zoom in," said Ellis.

The image on the screen froze and then slowly zoomed in on Lucy until her face filled the right-hand side of the screen.

Ellis stared at the faces of the two women on the screen, the warmth of the medicine's effects replaced by a deep, aching loss.

A buzzing came from the control panel beneath the screen and an LED turned red.

Ellis tapped it. The light stayed on. "Are you seeing any—"

Warning. Collision imminent.

He barely had time to grab the edge of the console before a heavy grinding sound ripped through the belly of the ship. He was thrown sideways, the movement almost hurling him out of his seat. The shriek of tearing metal reverberated through the bridge. A red light above the door to his cabin strobed. There was the hiss of pressurized air being vented. A siren started up, pulsing in time to the flashing light.

"Status report!"

Diagnostics scan in progress. Initial readings indicate a collision with debris of indeterminate origin and composition. Localized structural damage. Self-repair systems have been deployed.

"Localized to where?"

Sensors suggest extensive damage to the midship computing center. Additional damage to forward hull.

A low-pitched metallic groan echoed beneath Ellis's feet. The floor shuddered. A bank of lights on the control panel changed from green to red.

"Any more debris out there?"

There was a pause. More hissing came from the direction of his quarters. The red lights turned green again.

Unknown. Damage to internal and external sensor arrays has resulted in minimal environment-scanning ability.

Ellis tapped the screen on the control panel. A map of the ship appeared. Three patches of red marred the outer edge—two along the right-hand side near the main computer systems, the third on the front-right corner. That one was a direct hit on his cabin.

"Dammit! Okay, full stop."

Initiating deceleration sequence.

"What's the status of my cabin?"

A significant pressure drop has been detected.

"Which means what, exactly?"

There is a high likelihood of interior damage.

"Is the locker intact?"

Unknown. Internal sensors currently operating at three percent.

"Any danger to the rest of the ship?"

Unknown. Internal sensors currently operating at three percent.

"Okay, the ship's broken. I get it. Turn that damn siren off!"

The siren cut out, revealing the dull throb of the engines as they slowed the ship.

Ellis looked toward the red flashing light above the cabin door. Each pulse hammered a tiny ice pick into the center of his skull, between his eyes. "And the light."

The light flashed twice more, then stopped.

Ellis tapped his hand against his thigh. His right foot bounced up and down on the chair's footrest. After a few seconds, he stood and went over to the cabin. "Okay, let me take a look." He tapped the control panel beside the door.

Access to the pilot's quarters is not permitted. Internal pressure within the cabin is now at eight percent of expected range.

"And opening the door would depressurize the bridge?"

Correct.

"Any damage in the crypt? Wait, don't tell me. Unknown."

Correct. Internal sensors—

"Yeah, yeah. I understood the first time." He pointed to the bank of lights on the console that had turned red. "What do those lights mean? Bank 4A."

Bank 4A denotes the sensor array within the cargo hold.

"Those lights turned red just after the impact. Why?"

Unknown.

"Bring up the cargo hold camera."

The display flickered, but instead of showing the pods, the screen turned to a solid block of magenta.

"The camera's down?"

Correct.

Ellis pressed his fingers against the point where the ice

pick had entered his skull. "Of course it is." He shook his head. "Can you at least tell me whether I can make a manual inspection?"

Damage appears to be limited to exterior and directly adjacent areas. At this time, there is no indication of a hull breach in the cargo hold or the main corridor.

The rumble of the engines faded, leaving behind a hollow silence.

Ship velocity now zero.

"Any estimate on how long before the systems are back up?"

Current estimate is twenty-seven hours, forty minutes. Margin of error plus/minus thirty-seven percent.

Ellis let his head drop down onto the control panel. It landed with a dull thump that did nothing to shift the pain within. The familiar whine of the tinnitus rose into his consciousness. Groaning, he raised his head and looked toward his cabin. The light above the door was still red. He gritted his teeth, then sighed. "I'm going to check the crypt. Let me know if any of those unknowns become knowns."

Yes, Pilot Osako.

"And get that breach in my cabin fixed."

Yes, Pilot Osako.

5

THE CARGO HOLD TOOK UP THE BULK OF THE SHIP. APART from the bridge and the tiny living quarters, there was just a narrow corridor that led to a solitary airlock and the hold itself. There weren't even any lifeboats. In the event of an emergency, the bridge and cabin module could be detached, but it had no engines. If anything major went wrong, he'd probably be better off strapping himself into one of the pods. At least they were guaranteed to be airtight, and he suspected Trigenics considered them more valuable than the ship's lone pilot.

Ellis stopped off at the airlock and climbed into one of the lightweight EVA suits. He carried the helmet down the corridor to the entrance to the hold.

The lights on the door panel were green, indicating the cargo hold was safe. Given the state of the ship's systems, he didn't exactly trust the lights. He pulled on the helmet and flicked a switch on the chest plate. There was a hiss, and the helmet filled with oxygen. The helmet silenced the creaks and groans of the ship and seemed to amplify the tinnitus to a level that was almost impossible to ignore. He tapped the *open door* icon. A metal grinding sound came from somewhere inside the wall and the door shuddered open.

Most of the LED strips in the ceiling were still working. One bank, on the left-hand side, had failed, creating a dark patch over a few of the pods. He could see why the camera wasn't working. It hung askew on its mount. The green light on the top should have been blinking, but it had gone out. He walked over to the left-hand side of the room, beneath the camera. The mounting bracket was twisted, and one of the bolts that held it in place was lying on the floor. He picked it up, rolling it in his fingers. It felt icy cold.

Ellis slipped the bolt into his jacket pocket. The patch of darkness was at the other end of the room. He stared at it. His breath sounded harsh inside the helmet. A growing sense of unease made him turn away and walk across to the opposite side of the room.

He made his way up and down the rows, stopping at each pod. The LEDs were all green, but Ellis crouched and ran his fingers around the edges of each one to check the seal anyway. He'd already discovered three of his "passengers" had died of particularly virulent contagions. Protocols were in place to make sure any infections were neutralized, but he had no intention of testing the efficacy of that process.

The patch of darkness seemed to hang at the corner of his vision. He made a point of not looking at it, and when he got to the start of the last row, he almost decided to assume the rest of the pods were intact and head back to the bridge.

"Lisa, how are those repairs coming?"

Internal sensors are now operating at eleven percent efficiency. Preliminary self-repairs are underway. Current estimate for a return to full operating capacity is twenty-nine hours, seven minutes. Margin of error plus/minus twenty-three percent.

"So, the estimate went up, but now you're more confident it's right?"

Correct.

The tinnitus grew stronger for a few seconds, then died back down to a volume that was slightly above its previous level.

"Anything we can do to speed up the repairs? Redirect some power from the toilet or something?"

Negative. The energy requirements of the waste disposal system are dependent on usage patterns.

"What if I hold it in? Never mind."

Ellis let out a slow breath. The helmet redirected some of it across his face, and he caught the bitter tang of a mouth that hadn't seen toothpaste for several days.

His knees cracked as he crouched beside the next pod. Ignoring the bright green LED, he ran his fingers along the edge of the container. The seal was intact. He thumped the side of the lid for good measure, then moved on to the next one.

As he approached the patch of blackness, he kept his eyes lowered and focused on the pods. Without really knowing why, his inspections became slower and more careful the closer he got to the broken lighting.

There were three containers in the dark area. Some of the light from the LED banks on either side spilled over them, but the rest were swallowed up as though a cloud of some invisible light-absorbing material hung above those particular pods.

The LED on the first container, number sixteen, shone clearly in the gloom. He briefly considered trusting the sensors this time, just to get things over with, then forced himself to kneel and check the seal. It was still intact.

He stood and moved on to number fifteen, knowing

what he'd find. The LED would be red, and the container's lid would be knocked aside to reveal Tenshi's rotting corpse.

The LED was green. His hands shook as he ran them around the edge of the container, whether from stress or lack of medicine, he couldn't be sure. He checked the seal twice, then shoved the lid, trying to dislodge it. The pod remained intact.

Ellis let out a slow breath as he stood. As soon as he moved past pod fifteen, his uneasiness began to fade. The LED on fourteen was green, too, and when he checked the seal, it was undamaged.

The remaining pods stretched out in front of him. Each one was marked by a green LED. Now he was out of the dark patch, Ellis moved quickly again. He checked the seal on each container carefully but with no real expectation that it would be broken.

When he got to the end of the row, he unclipped his helmet and raised it a couple of inches. The air in the hold had a burned edge to it, but seemed breathable. He removed the helmet and clipped it to his belt.

"Lisa, it seems like the crypt is pretty much intact. The camera took a hit somehow and one of the LED banks is down, but the pods are still sealed. You can reduce the priority of repairs to this section of the ship. These guys won't care."

Understood.

Ellis rubbed his temples. A dull throbbing, fueled by the whining in his ears, had taken up residence deep inside his skull. Time for some medicine. He walked back toward the entrance to the hold. The LED on fifteen was still green. As he reached the door, he turned back. The room seemed less oppressive now. Even the patch of darkness seemed brighter.

He tapped the door control. There was a low-pitched buzz and the LED on the panel turned red. Frowning, Ellis tapped the screen again. Another buzz. The sound seemed to exacerbate the ringing in his ears.

"Lisa, I need you to unlock the door to the crypt. The panel's not working."

The tinnitus rose on a wave, drowning out the computer's reply. The LED remained red.

"Lisa, open the cargo hold door."

If there was a reply, the ringing in his ears swallowed it up completely.

A spike of pain jammed itself into Ellis's forehead. He cried out, grabbing his head and dropping to his knees. "Lisa!" The door in front of him stayed resolutely closed.

Waves of pain washed over him. Blood dripped from his nose and splashed against the gray metal floor. The world swam. The ringing in his ears ebbed and flowed, coming back stronger with each passing wave. Ellis crushed his hands against his ears. He fell onto his side. The lights seemed to flicker, and then darkness overwhelmed him.

6

Cold.

Ice pressed against Ellis's cheek.

Slowly, he opened his eyes.

A face swam in front of him. The pressure on his cheek disappeared. He blinked, dragging the face into focus. The woman from pod fifteen, Tenshi Kuro, stared down at him.

Adrenaline flooded his system, setting his heart racing and sending cold fingers of dread down his spine. He kicked out, pushing himself away from the woman until his back slammed hard against the reassuring metal of the door. "What are you doing? How..."

Tenshi took a step back. She was wearing a white jumpsuit that crackled like plastic as she moved. There was fear in her eyes. She glanced nervously left and right as though searching for a way out. At the other end of the cargo hold, the bank of LED lights were still out but Ellis could see the silhouette of pod fifteen was different to the rest. The lid had been removed.

He looked back at Tenshi, holding her wide-eyed gaze.

Looking at her set his heart aching. "I-I'm sorry. You caught me off guard. You don't need to be afraid."

Tenshi frowned, and Ellis realized he wasn't even sure that she could understand him. He knew a little bit of Denian, but only enough to get the medicine he needed. He held up his hands, palms toward her. She flinched a little.

"Can you understand me?"

The woman nodded, hesitantly.

"Okay, good. That's good. You're Tenshi, right?"

She opened her mouth as if to speak but the only sound that came out was a harsh whisper. She tried again, and this time managed to form the word.

"Y-yes."

Ellis felt a twinge of disappointment. He'd known the woman's name but part of him had hoped for a different answer.

He smiled. There were so many questions. Where should he start? Where *could* he start? Tenshi smiled hesitantly back at him, and the ache in his heart deepened.

"I'm going to stand up, okay?"

Tenshi took a half step backward, but nodded.

Trying not to move too quickly, Ellis got to his feet. He smiled again. "Are you hurt?"

Tenshi shook her head. There were dark smudges under her eyes, and her white jumpsuit only served to accentuate her pale complexion.

"Good. Are you tired? Do you need some rest?" Ellis almost slapped his forehead the moment the words were out. "No, of course not."

Tenshi glanced over her shoulder, toward the pods.

"We need to go." Her voice was a whisper, but he could sense the fear beneath it.

"Sure, okay. I just need to..." He hesitated, trying to work out how to explain Lisa. "I'm going to talk to someone else so don't be surprised if you hear another voice, okay?"

Tenshi nodded.

"Lisa, can you get the door to the cryp— to the cargo hold open?"

The door slid open, but Lisa didn't reply.

"Lisa?"

Yes, Pilot Osako.

Ellis felt a sudden surge of unexpected relief at hearing the computer's voice. He glanced at Tenshi. "I'm coming back to the bridge. We have company."

Understood.

He moved to one side and directed Tenshi toward the door. She peered through as though she was expecting an ambush. When none presented itself, she walked through the door, keeping as far away from Ellis as she could.

He let her get a few feet down the corridor before following her. The door slid smoothly shut behind him. There was a soft click as the locking mechanism latched.

With the door closed, Tenshi's mood seemed to change. The fear had gone, replaced by a look of intense sorrow. "I'm sorry."

Puzzled, Ellis frowned. "Why? What have you got to be sorry about?"

"I can't protect you."

"From what? We're the only people on the ship."

Tenshi looked toward the cargo hold door. The fear returned to her face, just for an instant. She smiled at him, but it looked forced.

"Come on," Ellis said, "let's get you warmed up."

They were halfway to the bridge when he realized the throbbing in his skull and the tinnitus were gone.

Tenshi followed Ellis onto the bridge. When she saw her own image on the main display, she frowned.

Ellis saw the look on her face and hurried to turn off the display. "Yeah, um, I was just... passing the time."

Tenshi looked at him and gave him a half smile. She crossed her arms and rubbed her shoulders.

Ellis ran his fingers through his hair. "You look cold."

She nodded.

"There's a shower, if you'd like one. The water's pretty hot."

"Thank you."

Ellis took a step toward the door to his quarters, then remembered the collision.

"Lisa, how are those repairs to my suite going?"

Hull integrity has been restored. Air pressure and composition are normal.

"Great."

He tapped the control panel. The door slid smoothly open to reveal the aftermath of explosive decompression. The foam on the bunk was almost completely gone—the only piece that had survived was a chunk snagged on a twisted fragment of metal. The locker had been torn from the wall. Its battered remains lay beside the metal bunk. The shredded corner of a jacket peeked out from beneath the locker. Chunks of broken mirror were strewn across the cabin. The poster that had been tacked to the wall was gone.

Attached to the wall about two feet above the bunk, there was a ragged patch of metal. Thick welding, the precise, almost perfect work of the ship's self-repair units, ran around its edge. Beside the patch, a triangular piece of metal was embedded in the wall. It was another piece of the locker.

"What happened?" Tenshi said.

Ellis started. "Oh, we hit something, and it punctured the hull."

"This was yours?"

He nodded.

"I'm sorry."

Ellis tried to shrug off the damage, but his eyes kept being drawn back to the locker. Pulling them away, he opened the door to the bathroom. "Shower's in there. Green button to start it. Give it a few seconds to heat up."

Tenshi bowed slightly. "Thank you."

He pointed his thumb over his shoulder. "There should be a spare flight suit somewhere. I'll put it out for you."

She bowed again.

Ellis waited until she was inside the bathroom and the shower was running before he grabbed the fallen locker and flipped it over. The door was missing. One torn hinge still clung to the locker. The other was missing, along with the locker's contents. He couldn't remember most of what was in there. Only the wooden cigar box really mattered, and it was gone, taking his medicine with it.

He picked up the shirt that had been trapped beneath the locker, hoping the box was beneath it. There was a corner of the poster but that was all. The shirt was ripped. He tried to summon up the anger to tear it apart, but in the end, he just balled it up and threw it into the corner of the room.

The ship gave a slight shudder, and he tensed. When the patch on the wall didn't fall off, exposing him to the vast expanse of space, Ellis let out a slow breath and looked at the bathroom door. A dozen questions filled his mind, but he forced them away. It didn't matter who she was, or how she'd come to return from the dead. Maybe she was just a stowaway or had been in a deep coma or something.

The important thing was that she was there. He already felt calmer, just knowing she was close by. He felt fine at the moment, but the withdrawal would come. When it did, she'd help him get through it, he was sure of it.

7

ELLIS HAD MEANT TO GO STRAIGHT TO THE AIRLOCK TO GRAB one of the flight suits for Tenshi, but instead he went back to the cargo hold. He tapped the control panel, and the door slid open, but he hesitated before going in. He still wasn't sure he wanted to know how Tenshi had ended up walking around the ship. The lighting panel was still out, but he could see the silhouette of pod fifteen with its lid propped beside it. A nervous feeling settled in the pit of his stomach.

"Stop being an idiot. She's just a stowaway."

He forced his feet to carry him into the hold. The door hissed closed behind him. He had to resist the urge to turn around and make sure it was going to open again when he was ready to leave. Two more lighting panels had died, creating fresh patches of darkness. He chose a route that would take him to pod fifteen without passing beneath the broken LEDs.

His footsteps echoed around the bay as he walked between the pods. He checked the panels as he passed. All of them were sealed, apart from number fifteen. The lid had been removed and propped against the side of the pod. The

LED on the control panel glowed red in the darkness. The lid was unmarked. No scratch marks, no broken fingernails, no smears of blood where its inhabitant had fought to escape.

For some reason, he'd expected to find the pod interior lined with silk cushioning, but what he found made a lot more sense. It contained a dense, foam material with a shape cut into it—the shape of a human body. From its size, Tenshi would fit in the cutout perfectly. It was probably custom made to protect her body from damage if the container was dropped or otherwise mistreated.

The sensors that monitored the pod's internal state were at the foot of the container—two discreet black rectangles. Ellis pulled them up and out. The wiring seemed intact, and there were no obvious signs of damage. The foam insert was fine, too. It was as though Tenshi had simply woken up, pushed the lid off her pod, and calmly climbed out.

8

ELLIS SAT IN THE PILOT'S CHAIR, HIS FINGERS TAPPING AGAINST the armrest. The soft rush of the shower faded away and a few seconds later, with a click, the bathroom door opened. He'd laid out a clean flight suit he'd retrieved from the airlock. It would be too big, but it was better than the clothes Tenshi had been... What had she been? She hadn't been buried; that wouldn't happen until the ship reached Kiran. Entombed? No, that wasn't right.

He shook his head, trying to ignore the resurfacing questions. The techs could work out what had gone wrong once they landed. In the meantime, he'd make Tenshi feel comfortable. She could have his quarters, and he'd rig up a bed of some sort. He wouldn't sleep much without his medicine, anyway.

The door to his room slipped open. Tenshi stepped onto the bridge. Her hair was still a little damp and clung to her shoulders. He'd been right: the jumpsuit was a little too big. But she'd rolled up the sleeves and pulled the belt tight around her waist.

She smiled at him. "Thank you. I feel... human again."

"Great. I have some rations if you're hungry. It's not steak. Well, it says steak on the foil, but it's synthetic." He grimaced. He was stumbling over his words like a love-struck teenager.

"That would be nice."

Tenshi's eyes sparkled. The shower seemed to have revitalized her, and her skin had lost its unhealthy edge. She still looked nervous, but it no longer seemed like she was about to run away and seal herself behind the airlock.

Ellis found himself staring at her. The resemblance had been uncanny enough in the photograph, but in real life, it was like looking at his past brought crashing into the present.

Forcing himself to look away, he pulled a pair of metallic pouches from a cupboard beneath the control panel. He squeezed and shook them both, then handed one to Tenshi. "It takes a couple of minutes to heat up."

They stood in awkward silence for thirty seconds before Ellis hurriedly slipped off the pilot's seat. "Please, sit down. You're probably tired."

"No, I'm fine. Thanks."

They stood, the uncomfortable silence returning until Ellis said, "Lisa, what's the status of the ship?"

Repairs are progressing at the expected rate. Current estimate for a return to full operating capacity is twenty-one hours, forty-three minutes. Margin of error plus/minus nine percent.

"What's the status of the external sensor array?"

A detailed examination of collision damage has determined that in-situ repairs are not feasible. I have adjusted the undamaged sensors to compensate with limited results.

He rubbed his forehead. That was bad. "Is it safe for us to get moving again?"

Forward scanning abilities fall below approved minimum levels.

"Any way you can get them above minimum levels?"

Negative.

"So... we either float here in the middle of space until someone finds us or we starve to death, or we carry on and risk hitting more space debris and being sucked out into—"

Suddenly realizing he wasn't alone on the ship any more, Ellis stopped talking. He looked at Tenshi.

She smiled hesitantly. "It's okay. I understand the risks."

"You've been on a spaceship before?"

"Yes, my father was a pilot."

The words caught in Ellis's mind and set off a dozen leaps of logic that all ended at one impossible point. "On Denia?"

"Yes, he worked for Trigenics."

More leaps of logic.

"Worked?"

Tenshi seemed to puzzle over her reply. "I haven't seen him for a few years."

Ellis could feel the heat from his food through the foil packaging. He wanted to ask Tenshi her father's name, but he was terrified of the answer. He'd have to ask eventually, but not yet. Instead, he retrieved a couple of sporks from the cupboard and handed one to Tenshi. She tore the top off her packet and squeezed it to open the end so that she could get to the food. The sight reminded Ellis of the envelopes that were now drifting out there in space somewhere. Thankfully, there was still no tinnitus and no headache.

He opened his own packet and shoveled a sporkful of food into his mouth. The synthesized meat was powdery and drenched in spices to hide the bland flavor, but he was suddenly very hungry, and the protein was welcome.

They ate in silence. Tenshi's face was unreadable. She was acting as though she escaped from a coffin and found herself stranded in space every day. The same couldn't be said for Ellis. Her comments had set his mind racing, and the ideas it was churning out swung wildly between terrifying and exhilarating.

By the time they'd finished eating, he'd decided to ask her the names of both her parents. That way he could be sure.

But she spoke first. "Who was the woman on the screen? The other one, I mean."

The question brought Ellis's thoughts to a screeching halt. "She... err." It was a simple question with a simple answer, but he struggled to find the words.

"Forgive me, you don't need to answer that."

"No, it's... it's okay. She's my daughter. Was my daughter."

Tenshi looked up at the now black screen as though the images were still there. Ellis could almost hear the thoughts whirring in her mind.

She looked back at him. "She's no longer alive?"

"No."

"What happened to her?"

"She was shot, accidentally, during a robbery."

This was usually where people expressed their sympathy for his loss, but Tenshi just tilted her head as though she was puzzled. "Is that why you're traveling to Kiran?"

Ellis started to say no, she'd died five years ago, but he stopped. He didn't remember telling Tenshi where they were going.

Tenshi dropped her eyes. "I'm sorry, that was unacceptable."

"No, no. It's fine."

Ellis searched for a way to change the subject and, without thinking, asked the question that he'd been too afraid to voice. "You said your father was a pilot for Trigenics. What was his name?"

She didn't reply immediately. Her brow furrowed as though she was trying to think of the answer to his question.

Ellis's heart quickened in the silence. When she did speak, the words knocked his world off its axis.

"Ellis Osako."

He clutched the edge of the control panel as a heady cocktail of emotions flooded his system—excitement, delight, fear, confusion. His eyes widened, and he stammered, trying to find something to say. "What?"

The word came out hard, sharp. It must have scared Tenshi because she took a step backward.

He held up his hands. "No, don't—I just." He reined in his rampaging emotions. "What did you say his name was?"

"Ellis Osako..."

The breath disappeared from his lungs. He felt his knees loosen and sat down in the pilot's seat before he collapsed completely.

Tenshi's face was still filled with concern. She seemed about ready to bolt. "I'm sorry."

"No, it's not your fault." He fought to find the right words again. Could he have been wrong, all this time? "What's your mother's name?"

Tenshi looked dubious, but she replied anyway. "Himari."

His world tilted again.

"When were you born?"

She frowned and inched toward the door.

Ellis tried to steady his voice. "Your birthday, when is

your birthday?" His hands were shaking, but it wasn't the withdrawal this time. If she said—

"May. The thirtieth."

With those three words, the doubt in Ellis's mind evaporated. He didn't know how it was possible and wasn't sure he *wanted* to know, but Tenshi was, somehow, the daughter he thought had been killed.

He laughed. "It's you. It's really you."

"I don't understand."

"I'll show you. Lisa, bring up the *Sept54* video again." He pointed toward the video playing on the screen. "Look, it's you."

Tenshi turned. Her head tilted to one side. The movement was so familiar, Ellis's breath caught in his chest.

She was frowning, though, her head shaking slightly. "It's—I don't know why you're showing that to me."

On the screen, the camera cut to the shot of Lucy standing beside the car.

"Because it's *you*. You must remember going to college?"

She shook her head, but he was sure he could see something in her eyes—like she was trying to dredge up the remnants of a memory from the depths of her mind.

"Think. Try to remember. Your mom and I bought you that car for your nineteenth birthday." God, Himari, what would she say about this? Could they be a family again?

Tears formed in Tenshi's eyes. She blinked them away. "No, I don't understand. I..." She looked at the door leading out of the bridge, toward the cargo hold. "No! I won't."

Ellis reached toward her. "Hey, it's okay."

She looked back at him, confusion and fear filling her eyes. "How did I get on this ship?"

Ellis waved the question away. "It doesn't matter. What matters is that you're here. With me."

The video reached the end and restarted. Ellis heard his wife telling him to leave their daughter alone.

"You said... You said your daughter was killed."

"I thought she—" The words caught in Ellis's throat. "I thought you were, but I was wrong. There must have been a mistake. We'll find out what happened. It doesn't matter, Lucy—"

"That's not my name!"

Tenshi slammed her hand against the control panel to open the bridge door. Ellis leaped from his chair and lunged. He caught her arm, but she twisted free as the door slid open and ran down the corridor away from him.

Ellis caught his shoulder on the door frame as he charged after her. "Wait!"

He gained on her quickly, but she reached the cargo hold and slapped the control panel. The door slid open.

"Lisa, shut down access to the cargo hold."

Understood. Access locks activated.

Tenshi slipped inside, just managing to get through before the door closed again.

Ellis slid to a halt in front of the hold. He pressed the open button. The display turned red and there was a short buzzing sound.

"Dammit! Cancel that request."

Understood. Cargo hold access locks deactivated.

Ellis pressed the button again. He was rewarded with a padlock icon and another dull buzz.

Most of the lights in the hold had died, but he could see Tenshi standing on the other side of the door. "Come on, I'm sorry. Let me in."

She stared back at him.

"Lisa, unlock this door."

Access locks are currently deactivated.

"What? That doesn't—" He hammered on the glass. "Please, Tenshi. Open the door and we can talk. I didn't mean to scare you."

Tenshi frowned and shook her head.

Ellis rested his forehead on the door and took a deep breath, trying to calm himself. He needed to take his time. Whatever had happened had left his daughter traumatized, that was clear. He'd freaked her out by unloading this on her without warning. He should have waited, gotten a psychiatrist involved or something. He took a deep breath and raised his head again.

Tenshi was still standing there. She looked so pale and fragile in the semi-darkness. Her eyes were wet with tears.

She spoke.

He couldn't hear her through the door, and he shook his head. "I don't understand."

Her lips moved again, and this time he managed to work out the words. "I can't protect you."

"What do you mean? You can't—"

There was movement behind Tenshi. A dark shape rose up in the gloom. It was humanoid, big and bulky, at least a foot taller than Tenshi and much wider. The figure advanced toward her.

"Look out, someone's in there!"

A second shape, this one smaller, appeared off to Tenshi's right. Ellis couldn't make out any features, but it looked like a woman.

"Lisa, what's going on? Who's inside the cargo hold?"

Cargo hold sensors are currently inoperative. Estimated repair time two hours and three minutes.

"Oh, for God's sake!" He mashed his fingers against the control panel. "Unlock the hold door, now!"

Access locks are currently deactivated.

Now there were four shapes inside the room.

He slapped his palm against the door. "Tenshi! There's someone in there. You have to get out!"

Tenshi gave a slight shake of her head.

He grabbed the edge of the door and tried to pull it open. His fingers slipped, and he fell back. "Dammit!" He punched the window in frustration. The blow sent a thunderbolt of pain down his arm.

The first figure reached Tenshi. It was a young man with a shaved head and pale, glistening skin. His eyes were closed, his mouth pressed into a tight line. His head was tilted slightly, and the bones in his neck pressed against his skin. There was something vaguely familiar about him, but Ellis couldn't place what.

The man moved alongside Tenshi and stopped. He was wearing a white jumpsuit, just as Tenshi had been. Ellis swept his fingers through his hair, then turned and ran to the airlock.

When he got there, the doors seemed intent on holding him back. They crept open inch by inch as though goading him. As soon as there was a wide enough gap, he pushed himself into the equipment room. It took him a few seconds to open the storage locker, find a toolkit, and fumble with the latch to get it open. The tools inside were old and poorly maintained, but there was a crowbar that looked solid enough. He grabbed it, turned back for a hammer as well, and then ran back to the cargo hold.

The man had been joined by a second, much older man and a woman with long blonde hair. They stood beside Tenshi. The woman's shoulder brushed against Tenshi's, but she didn't react. She just stared through the glass at Ellis while the others stood there, eyes closed.

More figures appeared out of the darkness.

Ellis let the hammer fall to the floor, then jammed the end of the crowbar into the edge of the door. The metal creaked and groaned as he leaned against it, but the door stayed closed.

Dozens of shadows moved through the room behind Tenshi.

"Lisa, what the hell is going on in there?"

Internal sensors are currently inoperative. Estimated repair time, one hour and fifty-seven minutes.

A girl, maybe twelve years old, walked in front of Tenshi. Part of her head was shaved, and there was a ragged scar running across her scalp. Her head was tilted upward and although, like the others, her eyes were closed, Ellis was sure she was staring at him. The girl's lips curled into a smile.

Ellis swung the crowbar at the window. It bounced off the glass with a sharp crack. He swung again. The tip of the crowbar embedded itself in the window. He pulled it free and fragments of glass tumbled to the floor. He swung the crowbar back again but froze. Another man had appeared and was standing just behind Tenshi. This one Ellis did know. It was the salesman. Marcus.

As Ellis watched, Tenshi placed her hands on the young girl's shoulders.

"What..."

A fresh tear ran down Tenshi's cheek. "I can't protect you."

The surrounding crowd moved forward, led by the young girl. They swarmed past Tenshi toward the door.

There was a beep. The control panel turned green and the door slid open.

The girl was through the door before Ellis could react. Her hand snaked out and grabbed him. Ice-cold fingers wrapped around his wrist. He twisted free and raised the crowbar. As he brought it down, a man with a broken nose threw his arm in the way. The crowbar thumped against iron-hard flesh and almost slipped from Ellis's grip.

The door was too narrow for more than a couple of people to get through at a time, but Ellis could see the figures beyond crowding forward to get to him. Hands grabbed at him. They pulled him forward, toward the hold and its mass of waiting arms. He swung his arms up to knock the girl's hands away. Someone else clutched at his face, hooked fingers grazed his cheek.

Blindly, he swung the crowbar again. It hit something hard, then was wrenched from his grip.

"No!"

Shards of ice wrapped around his ankle. The man with the broken nose collided with Ellis. They fell. Ellis's head cracked against the metal floor. Something hard dug into his back. Fighting to stay conscious, he rammed one arm across the man's chest and pushed. He could feel the chill of the man's skin beneath the thin fabric.

Ellis managed to force the man away and twist sideways. His shoulder caught something hard—the hammer. He grabbed at it. His fingers nudged it farther away, then found the rubber handle. He swung the hammer at the man's head.

It was a glancing blow, but it was enough to knock the man's head sideways. His eyes burst open, his face filled with shock and pain. He let out a high-pitched scream. Ellis pulled the hammer back and swung again. There was a solid crack as it sank into the man's skull. Blood spattered Ellis's face. The man slumped forward, pinning Ellis to the floor.

The crowd in the doorway surged forward.

Ellis felt hands clawing at his thighs. He kicked out, his boots connecting with something fleshy. He pulled the hammer free and swung blindly as he scrambled out from beneath the now-still body. Fingernails dug into his ankle. He screamed as agony tore through his Achilles. He kicked again, and the fingers let go.

The girl advanced toward him. Her eyes were still closed, but her smile had turned into a rictus grin that sent fear coursing down Ellis's spine. He got his legs beneath him and, ignoring the pain spiking through his leg, stood. The girl lunged at him. He knocked her hands aside and swung the hammer, but it missed and clanged against the wall.

A dozen people filled the corridor behind the girl. All of them had their eyes closed. All of them were trying to get to Ellis. Except Tenshi. She stood in front of the door, her face filled with sorrow, the mass of people flowing around her.

Ellis threw the hammer at the girl and ran.

"Lisa, open the door to the bridge and start evacuation procedures!"

The hammer clattered to the floor. Ahead, the bridge door slid open. The light in the corridor turned red.

Emergency evacuation procedure initiated. Priming sequence complete in fifteen seconds.

Ellis could hear the crowd behind him, the rustle of their jumpsuits, the slap of bare feet on the metal floor. He didn't look back.

Priming sequence complete in ten seconds.

The bridge seemed to be retreating with every step he took, but then he was inside and slamming his hand against the control panel. The door hissed closed behind him. He jabbed the lock button. The display turned red and a padlock icon appeared. Seconds later, he heard the dull thump of hands hitting metal.

Priming sequence complete in five seconds.

Ellis turned and leaned against the door. He squeezed his eyes closed, trying to force the image of Tenshi, of Lucy, from his mind. It clung to him, suffocating his thoughts. His heart was pounding, and he could hear the rush of blood in his ears.

Priming sequence complete.

A new voice made Ellis start. "I will, Mom. I promise."

He turned to look at the main display. The video was still playing. His wife was hugging their daughter.

Ellis clenched his jaw. He was safe now. He'd pull himself back from fight or flight and find a way to get to Tenshi.

"Lisa, what's the status on the internal sensors?"

Currently inoperative. Estimated repair time, one hour and fifty-one minutes.

"Anything you can do to speed that up?"

All options for expedited repair have been exhausted.

The thudding against the door stopped. The sudden silence did nothing to ease Ellis's concerns. He rubbed the bridge of his nose, trying to release the tension that was forming there.

His daughter's words filled the bridge again. "Oh yeah, the old man wants a hug, too."

"Kill the video."

The display turned black.

A metallic grinding sound came from somewhere beneath Ellis's feet.

"Lisa?"

Yes, Pilot?

"Did you—"

The control panel beside the door turned green, and the padlock disappeared. The door creaked and shifted slightly.

"Launch evacuation! Now!"

Launch initiated.

There was heavy clunk. The floor began to vibrate, and the roar of the bridge capsule's launch system filled the air. Ellis dived toward the pilot's chair. His fingers touched the armrests, and then he was thrown backward as the capsule launched. He slid across the floor and slammed into the back wall. His teeth clacked together, cutting his cheek.

He felt the bridge tilt forward. The launch system fell silent. That meant they'd cleared the ship. He fought to remember the emergency protocol. Did he have to initiate the distress signal? His thoughts were muddy and sluggish, scrambled by the blow he'd taken.

The capsule tilted again. He could see the chair a few feet away, but his vision was blurry. His head was pounding. Thick waves of pressure pulsed from his forehead. He reached toward the pilot's chair, but it seemed to recede as though it was actually pulling away from him. He dropped his hand to the floor and let darkness wash over him.

9

ELLIS FELT THE CAPSULE JUDDERING FIRST. THE REST OF HIS senses followed one by one. The faint scent of oil and grease from the metal grille his face was resting on. The taste of blood in his mouth. The outline of the pilot's chair against the glow of the control panel. The subtle, high-pitched whine in his skull.

Groaning, he rolled onto his back. His head was pounding, and when he reached up and touched his forehead, he found a lump the size of a golf ball that was tender to the touch. Blood was crusted beneath his nose.

"Lisa?"

His voice was dry, and for a moment, he thought the ship couldn't hear him.

Yes, Pilot.

"Status."

Evacuation capsule successfully detached three hours and nineteen minutes ago. Environmental support systems are currently operating at eighty-nine percent efficiency. Emergency beacon has been deployed.

Evacuation capsule? Memories reordered themselves

inside Ellis's mind until they'd assembled into a mostly chronological version of the events of the last few hours. He tried to sit up, but the sudden movement sent a wave of nausea crashing over him.

When the bridge had stopped spinning, he got unsteadily to his feet, walked to the pilot's seat, and sat down. Half of the lights on the control console had gone dark.

"What's the status of the Redhawk?"

Range to Redhawk seven thousand, eight hundred, and twenty-three kilometers. Telemetry link is intact. Auxiliary computing systems are operating at ninety-one percent capacity.

"What about the repairs?"

Current estimate for a return to full operating capacity is seven hours, thirty-one minutes. Margin of error plus/minus six percent.

The ship was still out there. Tenshi was still out there. Pain pulsed in the center of his forehead. He pressed his fingers against its origin.

"Are the sensors back up?"

Yes, Pilot.

The image of her standing in the doorway, people crowding past her to get to him, flared in his mind. No. They weren't people; they were something else.

"Do a sweep of the entire ship for life signs."

Understood.

Seconds passed.

No life forms detected.

"Recalibrate and re-scan."

No life forms detected.

Ellis's heart sank. "Any damage to the ship? Depressurization?"

The ship's hull is intact. Environmental support systems are functioning correctly.

He frowned. "Run diagnostics on the cargo hold."

There was a pause that seemed to drag on forever.

Cargo hold status is within normal operating parameters. Hermetic seals are intact.

"That can't be right. Recalibrate and check the seals again."

Again, there was a delay, longer this time.

Hermetic seals are intact.

"All of them?"

Yes, Pilot.

"Isolate pod fifteen and re-scan."

Understood.

Ellis stared at the control panel. The cargo hold status LEDs were dark.

Pod fifteen is intact.

"That can't be right."

All sensor banks are operating at ninety-eight percent efficiency. The likelihood of multiple errors occurring is less than .003 percent.

"Bring up the records for pod fifteen."

The display came to life, and the image of Tenshi appeared. Tears blurred Ellis's vision. He swallowed.

"Take us back to the Redhawk."

The evacuation capsule is not equipped with a propulsion system. Emergency beacon has been deployed.

Anger welled up inside him. "Then bring the ship to us."

The Redhawk is not equipped with remote piloting facilities.

Ellis let out a bitter laugh. He tipped his head back and closed his eyes. Tears escaped their corners and trickled down his face. The tinnitus rose in volume briefly, then faded again.

"Any response to the emergency beacon?"

Negative.

"How long will this thing keep me alive?"

Elimination of all non-critical systems will provide enough power to maintain environmental support for three hundred and seventy-one hours.

"So, two weeks?"

Correct.

A dull ache pulsed between Ellis's eyes. "Access my personal files and play file *Sept54*. Full screen."

Pilot, the additional drain on energy reserves will reduce environmental support longevity by—

"Just play the video."

The picture of Tenshi faded away and an image of a box-filled car took its place. A young woman was forcing a sleeping bag into the car's trunk.

Ellis smiled. "Are you sure you're taking enough stuff, Lucy?" he said, his words drowning out the tinnitus growing inside his skull.

ABOUT THE AUTHOR

Philip Harris is a speculative fiction author and video game developer. Originally born near Oxford, England, he now lives on the West Coast of Canada where he spends his days developing video games and his nights writing speculative fiction—anything from horror to science fiction to fantasy.

His first publication, Letter From a Victim, appeared in the award-winning magazine, *Peeping Tom*, in 1995. His published books include the *Serial Killer Z* series, *The Leah King Trilogy,* and an homage to the old pulp science fiction serials—*Glitch Mitchell and the Unseen Planet.*

His short fiction has appeared in numerous anthologies and magazines including *The Jurassic Chronicles*, *Tales from the Canyons of the Damned*, *Bones*, *Uncommon Minds*, and *The Anthology of European SF.*

He has also worked as security for Darth Vader.

For up-to-date information on new releases, free ebooks, and other exclusive extras, please sign up to the mailing list at http://smarturl.it/PodNews.

www.solitarymindset.com
philip.harris@solitarymindset.com

ALSO BY PHILIP HARRIS

Serial Killer Z

Serial Killer Z: Infection

Serial Killer Z

Serial Killer Z: Sanctuary

Serial Killer Z: Shadows

The Leah King Trilogy

The Girl in the City

The Girl in the Wilderness

The Girl in the Machine

Glitch Mitchell

Glitch Mitchell and the Unseen Planet

Glitch Mitchell and the Lost Galaxy

Glitch Mitchell and the Island of Terror